One Present from

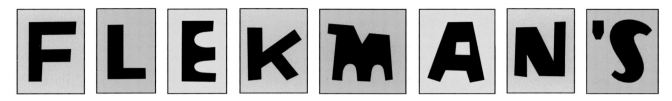

BY Alan Arkin   PICTURES BY Richard Egielski

HarperCollins Publishers

ALSO BY ALAN ARKIN

The Lemming Condition
Some Fine Grampa!

One Present from Flekman's
Text copyright © 1999 by Alan Arkin
Illustrations copyright © 1999 by Richard Egielski
Printed in the U.S.A. All rights reserved.
Visit our web site at http://www.harperchildrens.com.

Library of Congress Cataloging-in-Publication Data
Arkin, Alan.
  One present from Flekman's / by Alan Arkin ; pictures by Richard Egielski.
     p.   cm.
  Summary : Molly's grandfather offers to take her to a huge toy store in New York City and buy
her one toy, but he does not realize what a difficult time Molly will have making a decision about
what to buy.
  ISBN 0-06-024530-1. — ISBN 0-06-024531-X (lib. bdg.)
  [1. Toy stores—Fiction.   2. Toys—Fiction.   3. Grandfathers—Fiction.]   I. Egielski, Richard, ill.
II. Title.
PZ7.A687On   1999   98-20346
[E]—dc21   CIP
                                                                                AC

1 2 3 4 5 6 7 8 9 10
❖
First Edition

To Charlotte, without whom . . .
—A.A.

For Paula.
—R.E.

Grampa and Molly sat in the kitchen eating peanut butter out of a jar with forks. "Next Thursday I have an appointment in New York City," Grampa said. "If you come with me, I will take you to Flekman's."

"What's Flekman's?" Molly asked.

"You never heard of Flekman's?" asked Grampa.

"No," said Molly.

"It's the biggest toy store in the world," said Grampa.

"In the world?" Molly asked.

"Well, maybe there's a bigger one in China, but I never heard of it," said Grampa.

"Maybe I'll get some toys there," said Molly.

"Maybe you'll get one toy there," said Grampa.

"How come only one?" Molly asked.

"That's the deal," said Grampa.

"Maybe I'll see two good things," said Molly.

"Don't look a gift horse in the mouth," said Grampa.

"I don't know what that means," said Molly.

"It means one present is better than no presents," said Grampa.

The next Thursday morning Molly washed her face. She brushed her teeth. She carefully combed her hair. She put on a blue denim jumper and cowboy boots. She kissed her parents good-bye and took the train to New York City with Grampa. The train whizzed along. It passed trees. It passed fields. It passed small buildings. It passed big buildings. Molly looked out the window, but she thought only about Flekman's. Then the train went into a long tunnel and stopped. "New York City!" the conductor shouted. Molly and Grampa got out and took a taxi uptown, and there it was. Flekman's.

In front of the store was a man in a frog suit. He opened the door. "Have a good time!" he croaked as Molly and Grampa went in.

"Thank you," Molly mumbled.

Inside the store was an enormous Ferris wheel with frogs hanging all over it. They sang and jumped and croaked and shouted things at the customers. Behind the Ferris wheel were bears. Stuffed ones. On the floor. On shelves. On the ceiling. All over the place. There were stuffed camels as big as a house. Stuffed lions and tigers. Every kind of dog you ever saw. Stuffed dolphins and stuffed fish. Stuffed bugs, snakes, cats, and horses. Stuffed giraffes as high as the ceiling.

"This may take a little while," said Molly.

"That will be fine," said Grampa.

"I have to examine things very carefully," said Molly.

"I would," said Grampa.

Molly looked at the stuffed animals. She rubbed their fur against her face. She pulled their button eyes to see if they were on tight. She sat on them and threw them up in the air.

"How about a stuffed bear?" asked Grampa.

"Maybe so," said Molly. She tucked a bear under her arm and took it for a walk.

Then she saw a camera. It took seventy-five pictures. If you made a mistake, it talked to you and told you what to do.

"This is a good thing," she said.

"Very good," said Grampa. "You could get a camera."

"Maybe I will," said Molly. She took a few pictures of the bear.
She walked around and took pictures of salesmen. They smiled and
waved.

Then she saw the dolls.

They were talking dolls. Walking dolls. Wetting dolls. Sleeping
dolls. Raggedy Ann and Andys. Barbie dolls. Humpty Dumpty dolls,
Rumpelstiltskin dolls, Pinocchio dolls. Dolls who drank from a bottle
and burped. Dolls who fell down and cried. Even some very nice dolls
that just stayed limp and did nothing.

"Maybe a doll," said Molly.

"Don't you have one already?" asked Grampa.

"It's good to have a few," said Molly. She found a doll with a
beautiful face and long brown hair.

"That's the perfect thing," said Grampa.

"It could be," said Molly. She tucked the doll under one arm, put the bear under the other arm, hung the camera around her neck, and went to find the games.

"Where are you taking all those things?" Grampa asked.

"This is the problem," said Molly. "The bear is cuddly, but not pretty like the doll. I can take pictures with the camera, but the games are good for making noise and running around. Maybe I should get a *few* toys."

"Wait a minute," said Grampa. "We had a deal. We came here to get one present, not to buy out the whole store. You have to save something for someone else."

"Okay, okay," said Molly. She put back the doll. She put back the bear and the camera and looked around some more.

The game section was very good. There were indoor games. Outdoor games. Games to play alone, games to play with other people. Loud games and quiet games. Games that were serious. Games that were stupid.

A saleslady came over.

"Can I help you?" she said.

"Just looking at the games," said Molly.

"Have you seen this?" the saleslady asked. She showed Molly Upsy Downzy Inzy Outzy. It had dice and balloons and lights. You had to pick cards and answer questions in a loud voice, then blow a whistle and run around like a crazy person. "It's my all-time favorite," said the saleslady.

"Let's get it," said Grampa.

"I have to play it first," Molly said.

"Play it at home," said Grampa. "Buy it here and play it at home."

"I have to see if I like it," said Molly.

"You can't fool around with everything in the store," said Grampa. "That's not the idea."

"Yes it is!" said the saleslady cheerily. "At Flekman's you can play with everything!" The saleslady, whose name was Louise, put the game on the floor, and she and Molly started to play. They screamed and yelled and blew whistles and popped balloons and ran around like crazy people. Grampa paced. He talked with a salesman about the weather. He snapped his fingers and looked out the window. After an hour and a half Molly won the game.

"What do you think?" Grampa asked.

"No good," said Molly.

"Why not?" said Grampa.

"Too boring," said Molly. She looked at other games. Boggle. And Bingo. And Backgammon. Then Beauty and the Beast, Parcheesi and Twister, Ring Toss and Super Mario Goes to Hawaii.

Loud noises started coming from Grampa's stomach. He looked at his watch. "Time to eat," he said. "Let's go get some lunch."

"I can't leave now," said Molly.

"Why not?" asked Grampa.

"Because somebody might come in and take the perfect thing I want."

"Well, why don't you take it before they do?"

"Because I'm not positive that it's the perfect thing," Molly said.

"If it's not the perfect thing, you won't miss it," said Grampa.

"Maybe it is the perfect thing and I don't know it yet," said Molly.

So much growling was coming from Grampa's stomach that people looked at him as if he was hiding an animal in his coat. He walked over to a salesman who was dressed like a dinosaur. "Where's the phone?" he asked. The dinosaur pointed to the hallway. Grampa called Carnegie Delicatessen. "Hello," he said. "I'm trapped in Flekman's with my granddaughter, and I'm starving to death."

"No problemo!" the deli man said. "Tell us what you want—you'll have it in two jiffies!" Grampa ordered pastrami sandwiches and pickled tomatoes and two egg creams. In two jiffies the lunch came. Grampa paid the delivery man and went to look for Molly.

He found her back in the bear department. She was wearing a pirate suit.

"I found the one thing I want," she said.

"What is it?" asked Grampa, eating his pastrami sandwich.

"This," said Molly. She pointed to a big black teddy bear. He was in a baby carriage. Binoculars hung around his neck. A radio was in his lap. In the bottom of the carriage were a Monopoly set and a pair of roller skates. And a Sally Astronaut kit.

"What's all this?" Grampa asked.

"My present," said Molly very sweetly.

"Seven presents," said Grampa in a loud voice.

"He needs the binoculars to see far away," said Molly.

"What about the radio?" Grampa asked.

"He loves music."

"And the carriage?"

"What if he gets tired?"

"And the roller skates?"

"Sometimes he has to go very fast."

"And the Sally Astronaut kit?"

"He needs to visit the moon."

"This is ridiculous," said Grampa, losing his patience. "Put all this back and pick out one present! It's not that hard! We had a deal!"

"Okay, okay," said Molly. She put back the radio.

"That leaves six," said Grampa. "Just get the bear and put the other stuff away."

"I don't want the bear," said Molly. She made a lemon face and pulled her hair into strings.

"Then get something you want!" Grampa shouted. People looked at him as if he was a mean grandfather. He pretended not to see them.

Molly ran down an aisle and around a corner. "Molly!" Grampa yelled, running after her.

He found her three aisles away carrying an enormous shopping bag.

"Here is my one present," she said.

"What is it?" Grampa asked, not trusting her for a second.

"This bag," Molly said. "I made up my mind."

"It's filled with toys!" Grampa shouted.

"It's one present," said Molly.

"You've got twenty things in there!" Grampa screamed. "We can come back some other day! Just pick out one nice thing! Is that too much to ask?"

"Everything is nice!" Molly called out. She dropped the bag and ran away. Grampa chased her again, and this time when he found her, she was sitting on the floor with toys piled all over her. Her eyes started to look like the eyes on the stuffed animals: round and staring and glued on.

"Molly, get up now!" Grampa said. Just then Louise came by. She pointed to her watch. "Closing time in ten minutes," she said sweetly.

"MOLLY! SNAP OUT OF IT!" Grampa shouted. He grabbed Molly's feet and tried to pull her out of the pile. "You have to make up your mind right now. They have to close the store."

Molly's eyes went back into her head and she got calm and sat up. "I know what I want," she said.

"What is it?" asked Grampa with a big sigh.

"Flekman's," Molly said. "I want Flekman's."

"You can't have Flekman's."
Grampa said. He put his
head in his hand.
"Why not?" she said.
"It's one thing, isn't it?"
"Yes, but it's the whole store," Grampa said
in very tired voice. "You can't have the whole store."
"I need it!" she shouted. She jumped on a counter and
started stamping her feet very fast like a tap dancer.
"Come down!" Grampa yelled. "Come down this minute!"
"Flekman's! I WANT FLEKMAN'S!" Molly shouted over and over.

"Grab her! Get her down!" one of the salesmen yelled.
Louise got a butterfly net and started swinging it at
Molly, but Molly ran from counter to counter
so fast that no one could catch her.

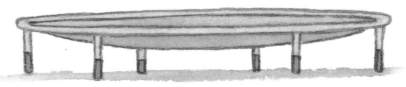

The manager heard all the noise and came running out of his office. He saw Molly running over the counters and grabbed a saleslady. "DO SOMETHING!" he called out. "WE'LL HAVE A LAWSUIT ON OUR HANDS!"

Salesmen started to chase after Molly from all directions.

Molly scampered over counters till she got to the playground section. She jumped on a trampoline, and it bounced her to the ceiling and she grabbed onto a chandelier.

"Call the police!" shouted the manager. "Call the fire department! We have a disaster going on here!"

Salesmen ran to telephones and called the police and fire department. "We have a girl swinging from a chandelier!" they yelled into the phones.

"Not again," said the police and firemen. They hung up, and in two minutes they were at the store. Policemen blew whistles and shoved everyone around. The firemen got big hoses and started spraying water on everything, including Molly, and she fell off the chandelier and into a net that Grampa was holding with Louise.

"Mine! All mine!" Molly said, her eyes bulging out of her head. She tried to run away, but Louise grabbed her and rolled her up in a blanket while Grampa went to the phone and called home.

"What's going on?" Molly's mother said. "You should have been home four hours ago."

"Molly is having a conniption fit," said Grampa. "We had to roll her up in a blanket."

"We'll be right there," said Molly's mother. "Meanwhile, call Dr. Brower. He'll know what to do."

Grampa called Dr. Brower. "It's Flekman's fever," Dr. Brower said over the phone. "My son Barry had it last year. Keep her calm, give her some warm milk, then take her someplace where there are no toys."

Grampa and Louise carried Molly to a quiet office in back of the store. They put her on a couch; then Grampa fainted. Louise threw water on him, but he didn't want to wake up. Molly lay very still. She watched the shadows on the ceiling for a long time. They made interesting patterns.

Later Louise came in. She gave Molly a washcloth to cool herself down with. Molly wiped her forehead with the washcloth. Then she put it over her face and let it sit there. She watched the sun make patterns of light through the washcloth. When it was almost dry, she took it off her face and held two ends and flipped it so it spun into a kind of eggroll. Then she opened it and spun it in the other direction, back and forth, one way and then the other, like a yo-yo. When she got tired of that, she took one end of the washcloth and used it as a kind of whip to swat flies on the wall.

When her mother and father came to see her, she didn't want to talk. She waved hello, then played with her washcloth some more. She made small knots in two of the corners and pretended it was a mouse. She knotted it up in a big ball and pretended it was a kitten.

"How are you feeling, Molly?" her mother asked.

"Fine," she said.

"Do you want a toy to play with?" her father asked.

"EHGGG!" said Molly.

She made knots in the other corners of her washcloth and fastened them behind her ears. The washcloth hung down over her face like a mask. She ran up and down the escalators and pretended to be a bandit.

Later Dr. Brower came over. He gave her an examination and said she could go home. "She's fine," he said to the family. "She has a touch of Flekmanitis, but it will go away. Just keep her away from toy stores for a couple of months."

Just then Mr. Curly, the manager, walked in. "I just heard of the magic washcloth that can do anything," he said. "Who's responsible for that?"

"I am," said Molly.

"You're a genius!" said Mr. Curly. "We want you to become the head of the idea department!"

"I have to go to school," said Molly.

"What about evenings and weekends?" asked Mr. Curly.

"Evenings might be a problem," said Molly.

"All right, all right," Mr. Curly said. "You strike a hard bargain."

So they signed a contract, and Molly went to work for Flekman's.
Soon she was known all over the world for her famous washcloth and
several other things, too.

THE END